The Treasure Hunt

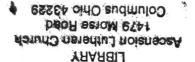

LITTLE BILL BOOKS FOR BEGINNING READERS

The Treasure Hunt

by Bill Cosby

Illustrated by Varnette P. Honeywood

SCHOLASTIC INC.
Cartwheel B·O·O·K·S®
New York Toronto London Auckland Sydney

Library of Congress Cataloging-in-Publication Data

Cosby, Bill, 1937-
    The treasure hunt / Bill Cosby; illustrated by Varnette P. Honeywood.
        p.   cm.— (A little Bill book)
    Summary: One rainy day, while his father listens to his old records, his mother polishes a silver platter, and his brother enjoys his baseball card collection, Little Bill discovers his own treasures, a loving great-grandmother and a talent for storytelling.
        ISBN 0-590-16399-X (hardcover) 0-590-95618-3 (paperback)
    [1. Family life— Fiction. 2. Heirlooms— Fiction. 3. Storytelling— Fiction. 4. Afro-Americans— Fiction.] I. Honeywood, Varnette P., ill. II. Title. III. Series. IV. Series: Cosby, Bill, Little Bill book.
PZ7.C8185Tr   1997
[E] — dc21

                                                                                        96-52072
                                                                                        CIP
                                                                                        AC
10 9 8 7 6 5 4   7 8 9/9 0/0 01 02

Printed in the U.S.A.   23
First printing, September 1997

To Ennis,
"Hello, friend,"
B.C.

To the Cosby Family,
Ennis's perseverance against the odds
is an inspiration to us all,
V.P.H.

Dear Parent:

One of the rewards of being a parent is seeing your children make discoveries about their unique personalities, interests, and talents. Everyone treasures those special moments when a child's face lights up with a flash of insight.

Such a discovery — "I really like the saxophone," "I've got a good sense of humor" — can spark a vocation or hobby that becomes a lifelong source of pleasure, especially when a child has a parent's support.

One way you can inspire your child is by encouraging her to explore a variety of activities — and by respecting her preferences even when she makes surprising choices. You should also take advantage of unplanned opportunities. As *The Treasure Hunt* illustrates, children often learn about themselves through interactions with others.

In this story, Little Bill is stuck at home on a rainy day. His father and brother both have hobbies they enjoy, listening to jazz and collecting baseball cards, but Little Bill isn't interested. Feeling lonely and bored, he retreats to his cluttered room, but he can't find anything to amuse himself with.

Great-grandmother walks in and saves the day. A wise and sensitive woman, she coaxes Little Bill to tell her a story. He makes up a wonderful tale about "something" that did "nothing" — he calls it "no big thing" — and his great-grandmother laughs and laughs. Little Bill discovers he has something special of his own after all: he's not only a good storyteller, he can make people laugh. You can tell this "treasure" is going to become a big part of his life.

It is gratifying to watch a child's sense of pride grow by leaps and bounds as he gains a sense of mastery using new skills.

Keep on, Little Bill!

Alvin F. Poussaint, M.D.
Clinical Professor of Psychiatry,
Harvard Medical School and
Judge Baker Children's Center,
Boston, MA

Chapter One

Hello, friend. My name is Little Bill. This is a story about me and my family.

No school and guess what? It was raining! And windy, too! What good was a day off with weather like this?

I walked around the house looking for something to do. In the living room, Dad was cleaning records. Everyone else in the world has tapes or CDs, but Dad still has those old plastic records.

"Listen to this," he said. "This is Dizzy Gillespie." Dad closed his eyes. "This is r-e-a-l music. Not like the stuff kids listen to today."

I knew what was coming next — a story I've heard a million times.

"I started collecting these records more than thirty years ago," he said. "This one is from my father. These are even older. These are by the jazz greats — Charlie Parker, Thelonius Monk . . ."

I backed out of the room as fast as I could. I can't understand why Dad thinks these scratchy old records are so great.

Chapter Two

In the kitchen, Mom was on a step stool. She was reaching into the high cabinet.

"Little Bill, please take this from me," she said. She handed down a large silver platter. "Be careful, honey. It's heavy."

Mom only uses it for holidays, but she polishes it all the time.

Each time she takes it down she tells me the same thing. "This platter was Alice the Great's, then it was my mother's, and now it's mine. Someday it will be yours."

I didn't tell her that when I saw the platter all I thought about was the turkey that went on it. I didn't care too much about ever having the platter. Maybe Mom should give it to someone else.

My brother Bobby came into the kitchen for a glass of milk. "You look bored," he said.

I followed him back to his room.

"Do you want to watch me sort my cards?" he asked. "These used to be Uncle Al's. Look! Hank Aaron, Willie Mays, Sandy Koufax, Roberto Clemente. You can look at them, but don't touch them."

I didn't want to touch them anyway.

Bobby laid out his cards and pretended to be a sports announcer.

"What a game, ladies and gentlemen! Roberto Clemente is on third base and Hank Aaron is at bat. Sandy Koufax winds up for the pitch and . . . POW! It's going, going . . . WAIT! Say-hey Willie Mays just ran a 50-yard dash! He's right under the ball! Ladies and gentlemen, this is great! Willie Mays has caught the ball and saved the day. Say-hey, Willie!"

I thought it was dumb to make such a big deal over cards with players I never even heard of. Those guys were playing ball before I was even born! Who cares!

Chapter Three

I went to my room and looked around. Everyone else had something special that he cared about. What did I have? I opened my drawers and looked through my closet. Clothes, books, a bat, balls, some games. Rocks. Crayons. Nothing special yet.

I was so busy that I didn't see my great-grandmother, Alice the Great, come into my room.

"What are you looking for?" she asked.

"There's nothing for me to do," I said. "Mom, Dad, and Bobby have special stuff to keep them busy. I bet you do, too."

"Of course, I do," she said.

"Great-grandma, what do I have that's special?" I asked.

"You're the only one who can answer that question," she said. "Think about it."

She sat on the edge of the bed. "I want to rest a minute," she said. "Tell me a story, Little Bill." "About what?" I asked her. "You make one up," she said. So I did.

"There was this *thing*. It was once something. But it turned into a thing. A something that did nothing.

"And so it was called no big thing."

My story didn't make sense. But
it did make Great-grandma laugh.
And she started me laughing, too.

"No big thing," she said, still laughing.

She kissed me on the head and walked out of my room.

My treasure hunt was over. I learned what was special to me—telling stories and making people laugh. And I have a wonderful great-grandma, who is very wise and who loves me very much. You can't polish or dust or sort my special things. You can only enjoy them.

I looked at the rain outside my
window and made up another story.

Bill Cosby is one of America's best-loved storytellers, known for his work as a comedian, actor, and producer. His books for adults include *Fatherhood, Time Flies, Love and Marriage*, and *Childhood*. Mr. Cosby holds a doctoral degree in education from the University of Massachusetts.

HOWARD L. BINGHAM

Varnette P. Honeywood, a graduate of Spelman College and the University of Southern California, is a Los Angeles-based impressive genre painter. Her work is included in many collections throughout the United States and Africa and has appeared on adult trade book jackets and in a children's book, *Let's Get the Rhythm of the Band.*

Books in the LITTLE BILL series:

The Meanest Thing to Say
All the kids are playing a new game.
You have to be mean to win it.
Can Little Bill be a winner...
and be nice, too?

The Best Way to Play
Little Bill and his friends want the
new *Space Explorers* video game.
But their parents won't buy it.
How can Little Bill and his
friends have fun without it?

The Treasure Hunt
Little Bill searches his room
for his best treasure.
What he finds is a great big surprise!